To:

Love:

INK

for all my little love bugs . . .

ethan, benson, michael, michaela, andrew, ainsley, clare,

jack, eliza, liam, beaux, nina, elias, will, & patrick. whew!

xoxo monica

LITTLE SIMON
An imprint of Simon & Schuster Children's Publishing Division
1230 Avenue of the Americas, New York, New York 10020
Copyright © 2010 by Monica Sheehan.

For information about special discounts for bulk purchases,
please contact Simon & Schuster Special Sales at 1-866-506-1949
or business@simonandschuster.com.

The Simon & Schuster Speakers Bureau
can bring authors to your live event.
For more information or to book an event contact the
Simon & Schuster Speakers Bureau at 1-866-248-3049 or
visit our website at www.simonspeakers.com.

Designed by Monica Sheehan
Manufactured in China 0414 SCP
First jacketed hardcover edition December 2013
10 9 8 7 6 5 4 3 2

Library of Congress Cataloging-in-Publication Data
Sheehan, Monica, author, illustrator. Love is you & me / by Monica Sheehan. —
First hardcover edition. pages cm Summary: Illustrations and simple, rhyming text
reveal that love, whether between a parent and child, best friends, or even a dog
and a mouse, is the greatest gift of all. [1. Stories in rhyme. 2. Love—Fiction.]
I. Title. II. Title: Love is you and me. PZ8.3.S543Lo 2013 [E]—dc23 2012051746

ISBN 978-1-4424-3607-7 (HC)
ISBN 978-1-4424-0765-7 (board)
ISBN 978-1-4424-4975-6 (eBook)

LOVE

is you & me.

LITTLE SIMON

New York   London   Toronto   Sydney   New Delhi

Love is me...

and love is you.

So when you smile, I smile too.

When you're around
the skies

are blue.

It's like being **happy!** times two.

Love is...

sweet.

And love is  G R

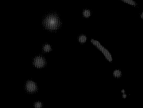
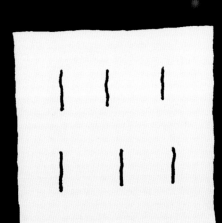

Sometimes love
is just holding hands.

It's a feeling

inside.

It's a smile

in your heart.

It keeps us
together

when we're
apart.

LOVE is

LOVE
lets you be

who
want

you
to be.

Love will catch you

when

you

fall.

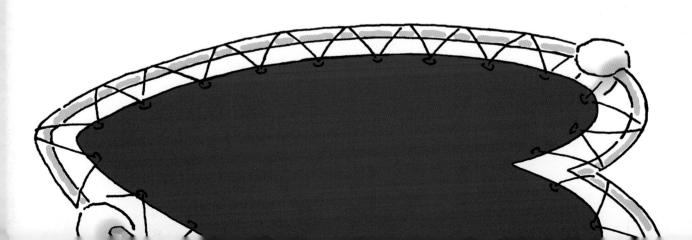

It's the **greatest** gift of **all**.

It's just us two...

without a care.

It's what we give...

and the times

It wipes away
the tears...

sends our **troubles** along...

Love is the place where you always belong.

And we've got love—me & you.
We're sticking together.

We'll see it through...
and wherever we go...

LO

will always be...

because...

love  is

you&me.